C000125598

A Cornish Retreat

Lily Wells

1

Lucy shut down her computer and grabbed her handbag from the desk drawer.

"Well that's me done for the next two weeks," she said as she gave Sophie the office keys.

"I'm a little envious you're getting away, but Cornwall in November, couldn't you find somewhere a little warmer?" said Sophie.

"I could find somewhere warmer, I just couldn't afford it," replied Lucy, "well not if I want to move into my own place again. Anyway the solitude is just what I need right now, some time to think and make some decisions about the rest of my life, maybe I can get it right this time."

"Don't be so hard on yourself," said Sophie.

"Six years is a long time to spend with someone and not realise who they really are. I'm obviously not a great judge of character when it comes to men, either that or I'm easily fooled." Lucy said as she took her coat from the rack and picked up her umbrella.

"People change you know," said Sophie.

"Do they, or did I just ignore the warning signs," said Lucy rummaging in her handbag for the car keys.

"And what exactly were the signs?" asked Sophie.

"How would I know, I was ignoring them," said Lucy smiling. "Anyway, from now on I'm going to decide what I want and then I just need to work out how to get it."

"Well don't forget to come back, we need you here," said Sophie, "the New Year rush will soon be upon us."

Lucy had always admired Sophie, her boss for the last eight years, she had worked hard to set up this business and then expand it until she had four offices across Bristol. Sophie had interviewed her just before opening her first estate agency; a small unit snuggled in between a greengrocer and newsagent in a neighbourhood that, at that time, was not considered a prime location. However Sophie had seen the potential and within a year they had moved into a larger place just along the street. Soon after that the competition started to arrive; there were now five agencies in the area.

She looked around the office with its light wood desks, comfy seating areas and uncluttered surfaces. Sophie had understood what people wanted – professional alongside friendly and welcoming. This was the kind of place you felt comfortable walking into even if you only wanted to browse.

Until recently she couldn't have imagined working anywhere else, she loved helping her customers realise their dreams. Whether they were buying or selling they were taking a massive step towards a new episode in their lives and she felt honoured to be part of it. Yes she had targets and they had to operate competitively but she always found that if the customer felt you were on their side, and she genuinely was, then everything else just happened.

Sophie's voice broke into her thoughts.

"I know things have been tough for you these past few months but your parents aren't in a hurry to move you out are they?" said Sophie.

"They're happy for me to stay but I need to get my own place again, first step and all that," said Lucy.

"I guess," said Sophie.

"Well I'll be off, you know what the traffic can be like on a Friday afternoon," said Lucy.

Sophie gave Lucy a hug. "Take care of yourself, and no running off with the waiter," she said laughing.

Lucy laughed, "I don't think there's much chance of that, I'm not even sure if anything's open this time of year," she said.

"Seriously, we need you here," said Sophie.

"As they say in all the good movies – I'll be back," Lucy said, she just didn't know if she'd be staying.

2

Lucy ran to her car battling with her umbrella against the wind and rain, thank goodness she had allocated parking behind the office. Her little blue Peugeot started with the first turn of the key, she listened as the engine settled into a gentle hum. With a tank full of fuel, packed suitcases in the back and her new burgundy notebook with its unlined pages safely stowed in the glove compartment she was ready to go. This was it, two weeks to decide what she wanted and then return to make it all happen. If she didn't do it now she would always be looking back thinking if only.

She selected one of her favourite CDS, a compilation of soft rock and modern folk, turned on the headlights and wipers, and pulled into the stream of traffic. It was bad enough getting out of Bristol without the added challenge of this relentless rain. As the windscreen started to mist up Lucy turned the fan up high even though the air hadn't yet warmed up, the cold blast made her think of warmer climes and air conditioning. Mark hated this weather, one of the reasons he preferred, or rather insisted, they holidayed abroad. Perhaps he was right, what could Cornwall offer that Corsica couldn't?

As she waited at a red light Lucy watched the pedestrians cross in front of her, each huddled in their coats, some hidden beneath an umbrella, none of them looking her way or acknowledging her presence. She had always loved Bristol and yet during the past few months it hadn't felt like home. She had begun to feel disconnected, perhaps that would change once she had her own place again.

It was another twenty minutes before Lucy joined the southbound carriageway of the M5, she moved into the middle lane to avoid the queue trying to leave at the junction ahead, not that any lane was moving that quickly - the line of red tail lights stretched out in front of her indicated it would take more than a few minutes to cross the river. As she moved into the fast lane a traffic report cut in informing her that an earlier incident had resulted in a build-up of traffic in both directions through Bristol, as if she needed to be told. At least she didn't need to worry about the time, the key to the cottage would be left under the doormat, something that seemed quite odd to her and yet perfectly normal to the landlady.

She glanced at the Sat Nav - 176 miles to go with an estimated time of arrival of three hours twenty-nine minutes. The route was straightforward - straight down the M5, pick up the A30 at Exeter and about two hours later take the coast road until she came to the cottage.

As the traffic eased she began to accelerate and quickly caught up with car in front, a glance in the mirror, a lane change and she was soon past it. At this rate she would be there sooner than expected. Accelerating and overtaking the car in front, no matter how fast she were going, was a habit she'd picked up from Mark. He had always driven like this and she had followed suit, mainly because when she drove he was always looking at his watch and sighing. Lucy felt irritated with herself, Mark had left some months ago and yet she was still following his rules - planning everything to the enth degree and then rushing to get there - even for this trip she had double checked her booking, put the journey into the Sat Nav, brought a map just in case, and even checked the weather to make sure she had the right clothes. November in England, she could have worked out what clothes she needed without checking the weather report. There was a time when she was spontaneous and happy to get up and see where the day took her, maybe this was one of the things she could change and perhaps rediscover that person again.

The rain had turned into a light drizzle, although it was dark Lucy was able to make out the well-lit industrial estates on the outskirts of the towns. They had grown significantly since she had last driven this way. Her journeys with Mark tended to be to an airport or to a city, rarely had they ventured into the countryside or travelled south of Bristol. He had always chosen where they were going, not that she had complained after all two weekends in Paris, a week in Tunisia, two weeks in Egypt and a birthday surprise to Venice was pretty good going.

Their last trip had been a weekend in Paris, ironically Paris had also been their first trip together. Second time around Mark had whisked her off one Friday evening, taken her to a tiny Parisian restaurant and proposed over coffee. Of course she'd said yes without even a hint of hesitation, if she was being honest she had mentally rehearsed this moment for some months. Mark had already chosen and bought the ring, as she expected it was a perfect fit. That weekend they walked along the Seine, stopped for lunch and discussed their future together, he had even suggested children. If anyone had asked she would have said this was the happiest moment of her life. If only she known then that two months later it would all be over. Lucy felt the tears sting the corners of her eyes.

Through the drizzle she could see a sign for the services, well this would be a first, she smiled to herself, stop for a coffee and take the time to enjoy it. She had never been allowed more than five minutes to nip to the loo and grab a take-away if she really had to. Mark had always wanted to get everywhere as quickly as possible, the journey was never part of the holiday. Well that was the first thing she was going to change. Lucy pulled into the car-park and stopped in a space next to a small convertible, she reached across to the glove compartment, took out her notebook and pen and stared at the blank page. She made her first entry on the pristine paper.

Enjoy the journey

Even writing it felt good.

3

Four long hours after leaving the office Lucy finally turned off the A30 and followed the road along the coast. The rain had started to fall heavily again soon after she left Exeter and, as if for fun, the wind had picked up to welcome her into Cornwall. She had committed the directions to memory, take the coast road until coming into the village, keep going for about 300 yards, however far that might be, and take the turning on the right, if she reached the church she had gone too far. Follow the lane for about half a mile, turn left and the cottage will be on the left. Lucy followed the directions and turned onto a narrow lane. Calling this track a lane was definitely stretching it, it was narrower than her driveway at home, or rather her parents' home, and the hedges were so close to the sides of the road that it would be impossible for two cars to pass. Negotiating this lane in the rain whilst trying to find the cottage was bad enough, reversing would be very near impossible.

Lucy strained her eyes against the darkness as she tried to find the cottage, she noticed the gap in the hedge and a wooden sign printed with the words *Hillview Cottage* just as she passed them. Gently applying the brakes she brought the car to a stop, reversed a little and drove into the driveway. She could make out the stone built cottage in the headlights, it was just what she needed right now – a place of solitude, a sanctuary, somewhere to think, no men, no-one advising her, no work, just her, her thoughts and her notebook.

She switched off the headlights and realised she should have brought a torch, the porch light was on but this didn't quite reach as far as the gate into the garden. Lucy grabbed her umbrella and handbag and stepped out of the car, immediately she felt the strength of the wind against her face as the rain lashed onto her cheeks. She made a dash for the porch and huddled under the overhang as she lifted the mat, as promised the key was underneath.

The cosy sitting room was exactly as she had imagined, in part fuelled by the photos on the website, a small sofa, a wood burning stove and a bookcase full of well read books. The woodburner gave off a gentle glow, in fact the room felt quite warm despite the weather. Lucy sat on the sofa, took a deep breath and started to cry.

4

Lucy woke to a knock on the door, the sunlight streaming through the window told her it was morning.

"Morning," said a dark haired woman as she poked her head around the door, "I'm Annie, I guess you're Lucy."

"Yes," said Lucy sitting up on the sofa. She realised she had slept on the sofa all night. She could only imagine how she looked, red eyes, crumpled clothes and probably smudged make-up. And who was Annie, the name rang a bell but she didn't recognise her which probably wasn't surprising as she'd never been to Cornwall before.

"You found it alright then?" said Annie "most visitors have to ring me, once then get to the road at the bottom their Sat Nav tends to tell them they've arrived at their destination," Annie laughed, "and all they can see is an old barn."

"Um, yes," said Lucy, "the directions," it suddenly dawned on her who Annie was, this was the lady she had rented the cottage from, "your directions were excellent."

"It is pretty safe around here but I'd lock the door at night, you're quite isolated up this lane," said Annie.

"I'm sorry," said Lucy as she stood up, "I must have been exhausted and fell asleep as soon as I sat down. Can I get you a coffee, I think I have some in the car." Lucy hoped she didn't look like she'd spent most of the night crying.

"I'll make the coffee, there's a basket on the kitchen table with a few basics and there's milk in the fridge," said Annie as she opened the door next to the sofa. "After that I'll light the woodburner for you. I'll be back every morning to get it going and clean it out if it needs it. All you have to do if put on the occasional log. It keeps the place surprisingly warm though there is an electric heater under the stairs if you need it."

"Thanks, I just pop upstairs to the bathroom," said Lucy as she looked around for the stairs.

"You must have been exhausted last night," said Annie laughing. "The bathroom's downstairs, through the kitchen on the right, you'll find a few toiletries in there."

Lucy followed Annie into the kitchen, the door on the right actually led into a tiny hallway with a staircase and then on through to the bathroom. Lucy shivered as she closed the bathroom door, this had obviously been added to the cottage at some stage and the heat from the wood burner didn't reach this far. It was a good size though with a large free-standing bath and a separate shower cubicle. She turned on the wall heater and filled the basin with warm water. A quick look in the mirror told that even though her make-up was a little smudged her eyes weren't red or puffy. Once she had freshened up Lucy went back to the kitchen.

"Feel better now," asked Annie.

Lucy sat at the table and picked up her coffee. "Yes thanks, and sorry again," said Lucy.

"No need to apologise," said Annie as she took a frying pan from the cupboard, "I'll make you some breakfast and then just talk you through where everything is. It won't take long," Annie laughed, "you've seen most of it already."

"That's very kind but you don't need to cook for me," Lucy protested.

"Nonsense, it'll only take a moment and you need something inside you, I bet you didn't have much on the way down here," said Annie as she took some eggs out of the basket.

"No, just coffee," said Lucy.

"There you go," said Annie as she put of plate of eggs on toast in front of Lucy.

"Thank-you so much, I hadn't realised how hungry I was," said Lucy as she cut into her egg.

"There's a file on the bookcase which gives you some basic information about the cottage, where the wood is and how to use the washing machine," said Annie as she sat opposite Lucy, "and there's some leaflets about some of the local attractions along with a couple of menus in case you want to eat out. There's also a contact number should you need anything."

"Thank-you," said Lucy. "I know I'm going to enjoy my stay here."

Annie looked at her quizzically, "I was quite surprised to receive your email, we get fully booked in the summer and sometimes let the cottage for a weekend this time of year. You are the first person who's wanted to stay two weeks in November," she said.

"I just needed to get away, and I haven't been to Cornwall before," said Lucy.

"It must be a man," Annie said.

"What must be?" said Lucy.

"The reason you're running away," replied Annie.

Lucy smiled, as much as she liked Annie she was not about to share her life with her. "Yes it's a man and I'm not running away. I just thought a break would be good," she said.

"I know, I ask too many questions, and, as you say, a break is always good. I'll get the fire going and put a few logs into the basket for you," said Annie.

"Thanks, a real fire, that'll be a first for me, it was actually quite nice coming into the warmth last night, a bit different from central heating," said Lucy as she finished her breakfast and put the plate in the sink.

Lucy followed Annie into the sitting room and watched as she placed a few pieces of kindling wood onto the fire, there was still a red glow in the bottom and it wasn't long before the first flames started to flicker. She then placed a small split log onto the burning wood and closed the door.

"That should keep going, just put another log on before this one burns out," said Annie. "I don't know what your plans are but if you need any provisions there's a shop at the end of the lane and if you want a walk along the beach just go past the shop, cross the road and you'll see a footpath that takes you over the dunes. There's even a couple of cafés open this time of year."

"I have to say it sounds idyllic, I think I'm going to enjoy staying here," said Lucy as she walked Annie down the path and said goodbye.

5

Lucy grabbed the car keys from her handbag and went outside. The wind was still up but the sun was shining. At least she'd remembered to lock the car last night. She unloaded the two suitcases and dragged them across the sandy driveway and into the sitting room. She decided it might be easier to unpack downstairs and carry everything up the narrow staircase, she could always put the cases in the cupboard under the stairs.

At the top of the stairs was a pine chest of drawers with hand-written labels hanging from the handles – towels, sheets and blankets. To either side were pine doors with ironwork latches. Lucy opened the door on her left, this must be the main bedroom. She closed her eyes and took a deep breath, the smell of wood polish and fresh flowers gave the place a homely feel, almost like being at her grandmother's house as a child, not old fashioned, just friendly and safe. The double bed was made up with blankets and a feather quilt, at the end was a thick woollen throw. It looked decorative however she suspected that she may well need this extra layer. This room was over the sitting room so it did get some heat from the woodburner but it probably got colder overnight. The bed was pushed up against the wall, she wondered how couples decided who had to climb over, tossed a coin maybe. Against the other wall was a wardrobe and a low chest of drawers with a mirror above. A vase of fresh flowers had been placed on the bedside table. If she was selling this cottage she'd describe this room as being full of character. She smiled, she felt quite at home here. Maybe she should consider buying a small town cottage rather than the open plan apartments she'd been looking at.

Across the small hallway was the second bedroom, a little smaller with two single beds nestled under the window and separated by a small chest of drawers. The beds were made up which made the room feel welcoming.

Back downstairs Lucy headed out through the kitchen door into the small rear courtyard with one open fronted shed filled with logs and some kindling, one locked shed for guests to use to store surfboards and bikes, an outside toilet, always useful, and a gas barbeque for those long summer evenings. She shivered and hurried along the path to the front of the cottage and took her notebook from the car. As she breathed in the sea air she could smell and taste the salt, she suddenly felt invigorated and decided that a walk would be good. It might help her think clearly. She had two weeks to make some decisions starting with where to live. She was incredibly grateful to her parents for letting her move back in with them after the break-up with Mark. Apart from anything else she needed their support, she had actually felt that her life was over. They had listened without judging her and without offering advice. And that had been the most important factor, she had been given plenty of advice - "find another man," "make him pay," "don't leave the flat," "cut up all his clothes," - all she'd wanted was to be as far away from him as possible. So she went back to her parents who just made up the bed, put on the kettle and checked on her every now and again.

Well that was all behind her. Today she would have a bath and go for walk, maybe the sea air would provide some inspiration.

6

In the short time she had been in Cornwall Lucy had become very aware of the wind. She put on her oversized jumper and some thick socks as well as her woolly hat. The extra layers meant she had to squeeze into her jacket, if she was going to start walking in the winter she definitely needed to buy more suitable clothing.

The lane was reasonably sheltered by the tall hedges however once she reached the main road the wind seemed to be waiting for her and managed to find its way through the tiniest gaps in her clothes. Lucy headed towards the footpath that would take her across the dunes and onto the beach. The sand felt surprisingly soft and dry underfoot considering how much rain had fallen the night before. Every now and again she had to step around bramble that was trying to encroach on the narrow footpath, no doubt this got cleared before the summer tourists arrived. The wind strengthened as she climbed the dunes, as she reached the top she could taste the salty spray on her lips. And then she caught sight of the sea. She watched wave after wave crash onto the beach and listened to the roar that filled the air, Lucy felt a real sense of awe at the power of this ocean.

She pulled her hat over her ears, dropped back behind the dunes and headed towards a lighthouse, Annie had told her she'd find a café if she went this way. Lucy crossed a small wooden bridge and took the steps that led up towards the cliff tops. The café was next to a small car park, she guessed people parked here and then made their way back down to the beach. Once inside and out of the wind she felt immediately warmer.

"Take a seat, I'll come and take your order," said a young woman as she picked up a pad from the serving counter.

Lucy sat next to a window and hung her jacket on the back of the chair.

"What can I get you?" asked the woman.

"A cappuccino please," said Lucy, "and a piece of carrot cake if you have it."

"We do, it's a customer favourite," the woman replied smiling, "I'm Sally by the way."

"Thanks, Sally," said Lucy.

Lucy looked out of the window, it seemed quite pleasant looking out from the shelter of the café, the sun was shining and the grasses were moving in the wind, there were few clues that you needed to wrap up well before venturing out.

She waited until Sally had brought over her coffee and cake before taking out her notebook and pen. The pen, rather than a pencil, had been a deliberate choice, her thoughts would become permanent. Even if she changed her mind during the next two weeks she would always have a record of where her thoughts had taken her and why. Lucy read her first entry - *Enjoy the journey* - then turned over to a fresh page and started to write.

Where to live?
The main priority is to have a place of my own where I can live my life my way. Living life my way is probably much the same as anyone else - eating when I'm hungry, staying in bed on a Sunday, inviting friends around and sitting up all night chatting over a glass of wine, and even choosing the colour of the curtains.

Lucy paused for a moment, if she was being honest she hadn't done any of these things in years, when she lived with Mark she rarely had friends over for late night chats as they had always done everything as a couple, and now she was living with her parents, even though they said she was to treat the place as her home, she felt awkward about staying in bed once they were up and about. And it was difficult to have friends over when her parents were watching TV. She picked up her pen again.

Having a place of my own where I feel comfortable doing what I want when I want even if I rarely do anything different from what I do now.
Deadline – end March.

She'd read somewhere that writing down a deadline meant you were more likely to do it. March was realistic as she should be able to sell the apartment she had shared with Mark, find a new place and move in by then. She started a new heading.

Location
City centre or outskirts?
Living in the centre will give me easy access to shops, cafes, and nightlife. It is also likely to give me the modern open plan space I love. Move a little out of the centre and there is likely to be an established community – could I fit in? If I lived in the centre on my own would I feel isolated? Which would be a better investment?

Lucy reread what she had written. At least she was asking herself lots of questions, in theory the answers should help her make a decision.

She wrote another heading.

Type of property
Apartment or house? One bedroom or two?
I've always preferred apartment living although I would like some outdoor space, even if just a large balcony. I'm not keen on a large house – why? Houses don't really reflect the lifestyle I think I want – professional job, trendy home, eating out. But is this really me, it was until a few months back. But now? A house still doesn't appeal, maybe because I can only see myself rattling around on my own in a house designed for a family – perhaps I could let a room.
Two bedrooms would be a better investment however it would also be more expensive. Maybe two bedrooms out of the centre would be more affordable. Is future investment important? How long am I likely to stay? Until I need somewhere bigger, perhaps when I meet someone else.

Meeting someone new, or even allowing another man into her life, was not something she had considered until about thirty seconds ago. Lucy was clear she was not yet ready for a relationship and yet, as she thought through her accommodation needs she realised that she had not ruled it out of her life entirely.

Choices – buy somewhere that I like in a location I want to settle in and is big enough for now
or
buy in a location I want to settle and is big enough for my future needs

or

buy somewhere that is a good investment with a view to selling up and moving later.

She reread everything she had written. Questions and choices. What she needed to do was make a decision.

Lucy went up to the counter and ordered another coffee.

"Here on holiday," Sally asked.

"Yes, I know this isn't the usual time of year to come down here for a break but I thought it might be quieter," Lucy said.

"It's certainly that, we get a few visitors this time of year, mostly coastal path walkers, but come summer it can be hard to find a table at lunchtime," Sally said as she handed Lucy her coffee.

Lucy carried her coffee back to the table and read through her notes again. As soon as the apartment was sold she would have the deposit for a new place. Her parents had offered to help if she needed it but she really didn't want them dipping into their funds, they hadn't even retired yet.

Of course she could move a little further out from the centre into one of the up and coming areas, where apartments were cheaper. This decision was going to be harder than she thought.

Two bedroom apartment, city centre, push budget, better investment.
Two bedroom apartment, out of centre, more for money, on budget.

Lucy thought for a minute and added.

House, out of centre, on budget, investment?

Oh well that's one decision not made but at least she had her options written down. Of course first the flat had to sell. One more entry for her notebook.

Sell flat.

Well that was a decision of sorts.

Lucy finished her coffee and said goodbye to Sally. It was still windy but she decided to take the path along the cliffs, she'd just stay away from the edge.

As she climbed higher she took in the views across to St Ives in one direction and towards the lighthouse in the other. This place must be quite something in the summer, as she imagined families playing together on the beach and couples splashing in the sea she felt the heat of her tears as they clung to her eyelashes. Come on Lucy, it's been nearly six months, pull yourself together.

She climbed down the steps that led to the rocks and beach below and sat for a while watching the sea slide off the rocks revealing pockets of sand and little rock pools only to come crashing in and reclaim them again. As each wave receded a little more beach and a little more rock were exposed to the daylight, the effect was hypnotic. Lucy could happily spend the rest of the day watching until the sea had given back everything she had claimed earlier that morning.

Although she was reluctant to move Lucy decided she had better make her way back, she had a few hours of daylight left but she wanted to explore the dunes. She took a hanky out of her bag, something her mother had taught her never to leave home without, dried her eyes and made her way back.

The path back along the dunes took her past some lovely chalets. One or two had smoke coming from the chimneys, most seemed empty. Lucy could see another café nestled in the dunes, she was feeling quite hungry, no doubt due to the long walk and sea air, and hoped they were still serving some light snacks even though it must be after lunchtime. Inside were half a dozen tables and a couple of sofas, Lucy was surprised that the place was half full with customers.

"Can I help," said a young man as he carried a tray and placed it on the table beside a young couple.

"Oh, yes, a coffee please," said Lucy.

"Any particular type?" he asked.

"Cappuccino," she replied.

"Coming up, though can I suggest our hot chocolate, you look pretty cold and it's guaranteed to warm you up," the young man said smiling.

"I'm not sure," Lucy said, she didn't usually drink the stuff, "OK I'll give it a try," she said thinking that maybe this was also a good time to try something new, even if it was only a hot drink.

"If you don't like it I'll exchange it for a coffee – no charge. My name's Jake," the young man said holding out his hand.

Lucy was a bit taken aback but she took his hand, "I'm Lucy," she said, "Do you have a menu?"

"The kitchen's closed but I can do you a sandwich or some leek and potato soup if you'd like something hot," Jake said.

"The soup sounds lovely, I'll have that," she said.

Lucy sat at a table for two beside the window, she had a great view of the sea and watched as the waves continuously pounded the beach.

"Here you go – extra marshmallows," said Jake as he brought over her hot chocolate, "the soup will be a few minutes."

Lucy smiled, "thanks," she said looking up at him.

She hadn't really noticed him the first time he spoke, he was taller than Mark, similar age to herself, and still sporting his summer tan.

"I haven't seen you around before, are you staying locally," Jake asked.

"A short walk away, thought I'd take a winter break," said Lucy.

"Great place to come, and quieter than summer," Jake said still standing next to her table.

Lucy took a sip from for mug, it was pretty good, she looked out of the window, hoping he would go away, he was nice enough but she wanted her own company.

"Do you like it?" he asked.

"Yes thanks, really warning," she said.

"I'll leave you to it," Jake said as he walked back to the counter.

Lucy gazed out of the window at the sea. She watched as the receding tide slowly exposed more of the beach. This was what she had been looking forward to, time to just sit and stare and think. In less than two weeks she would be heading back and she needed to have a plan. She couldn't stay living with her parents forever, she needed to be in her own place. She loved her job however she didn't there were any real opportunities for her, maybe now was the time to find something new. And of course there was the whole relationship thing. She hadn't imagined being with anyone other than Mark and now she wasn't sure if anyone else could fill the gap, or even if she wanted the gap filled.

"Here you go," said Jake as he brought her soup, "just what the doctor ordered."

"Thanks, though I don't remember my doctor ever prescribing this," Lucy said, smiling.

"Perhaps he should," said Jake as he put the soup and chunks of bread in front of her.

The soup was wonderful, Lucy was tempted to ask for the recipe but didn't want to encourage him, or anyone else, to sit and chat.

As she watched the sun slowly move over St Ives and towards the horizon she realised it wouldn't be too long before the light started to fade. Lucy finished her soup and looked around for Jake, he didn't appear to be about so she left some money on the table and hoped it was enough.

7

Lucy made her way back across the dunes and onto the road through the village. She had noticed the shop earlier, according to the sign they sold fresh bread, veg and coffee along with all your daily provisions. She walked through the gates and discovered the shop itself was housed in what looked like the end of a stone barn. When she opened the door a bell rang, very quaint she thought.

She had to admit that the shop was not what she'd expected. For a start there was no-one else about, the owner was obviously not worried about shoplifters, and it was tiny, about the size of a front room.

In the centre was a large table piled with fresh fruit, vegetables and a few loaves of freshly baked bread. There was narrow shelving around two sides of the room with a selection of dried, tinned, and bottled food including sugar, pasta and jam which, she noted, was made locally, as well as a small selection of wines and beers. A tall fridge and freezer were located next to the counter.

Lucy turned to the door as she heard the bell ring.

"Afternoon," said a young man as he walked into the shop.

"Hi," Lucy replied, it was cold outside and yet he was wearing jeans and a t-shirt. His t-shirt advertised the local surf school, something she wouldn't be trying out this holiday.

"I haven't seen you around before, on holiday?" he asked.

"Yes," she replied still having no idea who he was.

"I'm Sam," he said as if reading her mind, he held out his hand.

Lucy shook it, must be a custom around here she thought, shaking hands with new customers.

"I run this place, well actually my parents do and I help out in the winter," Sam said.

"I'm Lucy, I'm staying at a cottage up the lane for a couple of weeks," she said.

"Well you'll find most things you need here and if we haven't got it we will try and get it," he said.

Lucy scanned the shelves. "You sell books," she said sounding surprised as she saw the small row of books on the top shelf.

"Not exactly, it's a book exchange, great for everyone but especially holidaymakers. Finish your book and come and swap it for something else," Sam said.

"That's novel," Lucy smiled as she realised what she'd said, "how do you make money from it?" she asked.

"We don't," he said, "but everyone seems to like it."

Lucy smiled, this was a whole new world to her, going into a shop to swap things was something she hadn't experienced before.

She looked behind the till and noticed the coffee machine.

"We do coffee as well, you know, the proper stuff. You're only a short walk away so you could come down here for your early morning caffeine fix," said Sam.

"I might just do that," Lucy said. "Do you have any microwave meals? I'm looking for something quick and easy."

"Do you have a microwave?" Sam asked.

Lucy tried to picture the kitchen, "I'm not sure, I don't think so now you mention it," she said.

She looked around the shop. She actually enjoyed cooking she just hadn't done much of it lately. She didn't like to take over her mother's kitchen and she had tended to eat out with Mark. Maybe this holiday was a good time to start doing something she enjoyed.

Lucy selected some fresh pasta, tomatoes, onions, basil and a loaf of freshly baked bread.

"Do you take debit cards?" she asked.

"Yes, we do have some technology around here," he said smiling, "can be a bit slow though."

Lucy laughed. "Sorry, I've struggled getting a mobile signal today," she said.

"Sometimes it's good that people can't get hold of you," Sam said as he put her shopping into a small box.

"If you don't feel like cooking there are a couple of good pubs and one's in walking distance," he said gesturing to the building next door.

"Thanks," Lucy said.

"You probably won't need to book this time of year but when you come in the summer it can get quite busy," Sam said.

"What makes you think I'll be back?" Lucy asked.

"Everyone comes back sooner or later, I reckon you'll be back sooner than you think," he said.

"Maybe," she said as she walked out of the shop.

She'd only been here one day and already she knew that coming to Cornwall had been a good decision.

8

Lucy put her box of shopping on the kitchen table and went into the sitting room to put another log on the woodburner. She sat in front of the fire for a while watching the flames as they first flickered into life and then caught hold of the log, she closed the vent at the bottom just as Annie had shown her, the flames died down a little but still gave out a warming glow. This cottage was very different to her apartment, and not at all something she would have chosen for herself. It was cosy with tiny rooms, unlike the open plan she preferred. The sitting room contained a small sofa and one arm chair. There were a couple of foam cubes stacked in the corner to use as extra seating if needed. There was no room for anything else, Lucy began to wonder what else she would really need.

Once the fire was burning well Lucy started to prepare her simple meal. A quick hunt in the cupboards and she found the pans as well as some olive oil. She made a sauce from the tomatoes, onions and basil and poured it over freshly cooked pasta. A glass of Merlot and her meal was complete.

As she ate she started to think that one of the reasons she felt disconnected from the city was because she hadn't engaged with the community since moving in with her parents. If she was being honest with herself she hadn't engaged with the community when she lived in the centre with Mark. She'd had him though and they went out regularly so got to know people in the local restaurants even if they hadn't become close friends. What she wanted was to be able to walk down the street to get some milk and say hello to the people she met on the way. She opened her notebook and wrote:

Decision – out of centre location within a community with a high street that has shops and cafes.
Where?

She knew most areas in and around Bristol yet she didn't really know what it would be like to live in any of them. And there were other considerations such as how long it would take her to get to work. This was a decision she would have to make when she returned as it required a bit of research.

She put the notebook down. She had made another decision and that felt like progress. A little time and space was all she had needed.

After clearing away the dishes Lucy put another log on the woodburner and selected a book from the shelf. She hadn't taken the time to read a novel for quite a while. She'd actually forgotten how much pleasure there was in curling up on the sofa and becoming totally absorbed in a good story. Add the glowing fire to the mix and she felt she could really start to enjoy this quieter way of life.

9

Lucy stepped out of the bath, put on the towelling robe and wrapped a towel around her hair. It felt good to be able to have a long soak in the morning rather than rush around drying her hair, applying her make-up and joining the queues of traffic. When she got back to Bristol perhaps she could ask about working flexible hours, or even work from home once a week.

She heard the knock on the door as she walked into kitchen.

"Come on in Annie" Lucy called.

The door opened and Jake walked in carrying two take-away coffee cups.

"You're not Annie," said Lucy as she pulled her robe closer around her body.

"Well spotted," said Jake grinning, "I've come to light your fire, it's going to be cold tonight so make sure you keep it going."

"But you run the coffee shop," said Lucy still trying to work out why he was here.

"Annie's my mother, she had to go into Truro today so I said I'd pop in," Jake said.

Jake handed her one of the cups, "Cappuccino," he said, "the one you didn't have yesterday."

Lucy held onto her robe and took the coffee from him.

"Thanks," she said, "perks of being the boss?"

"I got these from the shop up the road, it was on my way and I wanted one," he replied.

Lucy took the lid of her coffee and took a sip.

"This is good," she said, "I could make this a habit," she said as the warmth of the coffee seeped through her.

"What me bringing you coffee for breakfast," Jake said grinning.

"I'll just get dressed, I won't be a minute," she said deciding not to respond to his comment, although the thought did briefly cross her mind causing her to smile.

Lucy took her coffee upstairs, pulled on a pair of jeans and sweater, and combed her hair.

"The fire's gone out," Jake called up the stairs, "would you like me to relight it now or put it ready for you to light later?" he asked.

"I'll light it later," she shouted down the stairs. Oddly she felt quite at ease talking to Jake even though she had only met him the once.

She was only gone a few minutes but when she got down to the kitchen Jake had already set up the fire and was sitting at the table drinking his coffee.

"Thanks," she said as she joined him.

"Have you seen much of the area yet," he asked.

"No, I've had a walk up near the lighthouse, that's definitely taking your life in your hands, it was decidedly windy," she said. "Today I thought I'd explore in the other direction and tomorrow I plan to go into St Ives."

"I could take you if you like. I've got cover in the coffee shop tomorrow. Anyway parking can be a nightmare, even at this time of year, so a little local knowledge could be in your favour," Jake said.

"That's very kind but no thanks, I don't want to take up your time," she said.

"It would be my pleasure, I could show you around and take you for lunch," he said.

As comfortable as she felt with Jake Lucy really wanted to spend time on her own. And she certainly didn't want the company of a man, particularly one she found quite attractive.

"Where do you want to go?" Jake asked.

"I thought I'd visit the Tate and explore the art galleries. I would say it was one of my hobbies but I haven't had much time for painting lately," she said.

"Excellent, I could take you to some of the hidden galleries and then we could stop for lunch, I'll pick you up at ten, I can see you're not an early riser," he said without waiting for her to agree.

"I'm on holiday," she said defensively.

"Great, it's a date," said Jake.

"Well I'd rather not call it a date but ten it is," she said smiling.

10

After Jake had left Lucy warmed up a tin of soup and poured it into a flask, she filled another with coffee, Annie had thought of everything when equipping this cottage. She cut and wrapped a couple of slices of fresh bread and put them, along with two large mugs and a picnic blanket, into a beach bag she'd found hanging on the coat hooks.

As she walked along the lane Lucy took a deep breath and tasted the salty air, it felt clean and fresh not full of the diesel fumes she was always trying to avoid. She turned her head slightly to feel the warmth of the sun on her face. Now the wind had dropped it felt less cold, not quite swimming weather but warm enough to enjoy the walk and sit outside.

Once on the footpath she turned left and headed across the cliff tops, warning signs suggested getting too close to the edge was not a great idea. She passed the closed lifeguard station with the telephone on the wall to use in the event of an emergency and the café where she'd met Jake for the first time. Perhaps she would stop for a hot chocolate on the way back.

Lucy found a sunny spot overlooking the sea, she spread her blanket on the sand, poured the soup into a mug and unwrapped the bread. There was always something satisfying about a large chunk of bread soaked in soup, so much better than the croutons they usually served in restaurants, OK they gave you bread as well but no-one dared dip it in public.

Time to make some more decisions. She reread her earlier entries – lots of questions and two decisions.

Sell the flat.
Live in a community.

She turned to a clean page and started writing.

Job/Career
I love my job but lately I've started to think that I need to make changes.

Lucy thought for a while and decided to list what she liked and disliked about her job.

What I like about my job
Working for clients.
Photographing the houses.

Lucy hadn't given this part of her job much thought and yet she enjoyed taking photographs that showed the appeal of each house, maybe she could do more photography as part of a job or even as a hobby. She continued to write.

Working with Sophie.
Training new employees.
Designing and running marketing campaigns.

What I would like to change
Being stuck in traffic when travelling to meet clients.
Have more control of the/a business.

Options
Stay where I am and ask for promotion or something that gives me a new challenge with more responsibility and control.
Move to a different agency.

Try an entirely different job.
Set up my own business – what though?

Lucy crossed out *Move to a different agency*, she realised this would not meet her needs. She thought for a while about setting up her own business.

What would my business look like?
Working with people.
Not too much city travel.
Estate agency?
Shop?
Photographer?
Bake cakes?

She smiled at the last one, she wrote it down because it popped into her head and yet she couldn't quite see herself baking, she was more of a front of house person.

Considerations
Financing a new venture – the only capital available will be from the sale of the apartment. My parents may consider loaning me the money although I would need to consider this carefully as I do not want to risk their future. Possibly raise money from the bank. Really need to have a business idea first!
Premises – most likely rent or lease somewhere, it might be possible to find somewhere with living accommodation. The idea of working from home has always had appeal so this could be the best of both words depending on the business.
Note – still need a business idea.

She poured a coffee and looked out at the sea, it was a clear day and she could see all the way along the coast. The blue of the sky and sea almost merged with just a feint line to indicate the horizon. Every now and again she'd see a bird circle above the water waiting for just the right moment before it plunged and claimed its prize.

Lucy watched the waves as each small swell slowly grew until it broke sending white foam and spray crashing towards the beach. She started to count the seconds between one wave receding and another advancing, before she realised it her coffee had gone cold.

As she packed everything away she started to think about Jake. She hadn't come here to find a new man, and yet, even though she had only met him twice, he was beginning to invade her thoughts. Maybe she was ready to start another relationship. She shook her head, in less than two weeks she would be gone, back to the job in hand, relationships were definitely at the bottom of her list.

11

Annie knocked on the door at nine-thirty.

"You look nice," said Annie. "I'll just sort the fire and then I'll be out of your way."

"Thanks," said Lucy, "I hope this weather brightens up, I can't believe how changeable it is."

Lucy felt a little embarrassed, she didn't want to give the impression she was trying to impress Jake and yet she had got up early to have a bath, apply some make-up and blow dry her hair. She had even changed her clothes although that was more to do with the weather.

Jake pulled up outside the cottage just before ten.

"You two have a great time," Annie said as she left.

Lucy grabbed her scarf and umbrella. She ran from the porch and jumped into the front seat of Jake's Toyota pick-up.

"How come the weather changes so quickly here," she said, "I expected it to be a bit chilly but where does all this rain and wind come from."

Jake laughed. "You do know this is one of the windiest counties in England, even in summer," he said, "if you're looking for hot, dry and sunny then I'd try the Med."

"I have tried it, and I liked it. Though I must say there is something to be said for this area, even at this time of year," said Lucy.

"I know what you mean, when I came back it felt like I should be here." Jake said quietly.

He turned to her. "You really should come down here in the summer, yes there are a lot of tourists but there are no fights for sunbeds, everyone is pretty chilled, and you'll find more going on," Jake said.

"I've heard that even the supermarkets open in summer."

"Very funny," said Lucy, "though come to think of it I haven't actually seen one, perhaps I need to get out more," she laughed.

"If you want directions there are a couple close by," said Jake.

"No, I'm happy with the local services," she said, smiling.

Jake followed the road into St. Ives and pulled into a small car park near the centre.

"If you come here in the summer you might be better off catching the train, car parking can be a bit of a challenge," said Jake.

"I'll remember that," she said.

"Come on, the rain has stopped, any moment now the sun will be shining, we can enjoy a walk before lunch," Jake said as he jumped out of the truck.

Lucy looked at the sky, as if on cue the clouds moved slowly apart and the sun made a hazy appearance. She grabbed her umbrella.

"Just in case," she said, laughing.

She followed Jake into a narrow street that led down towards the harbour.

Jake pointed to the cottages, "these are the old fisherman's cottages, that's old cottages not old fisherman, though they may have been old too. Nearly all of these are holiday cottages now, in the summer this place really comes alive, some days it can be difficult to walk and you definitely wouldn't want to drive along here."

Lucy stopped to have a closer look, "They have got a lot of character, narrow but tall, how many storeys are they?" she asked.

"They vary, some are four storeys with only one room on each floor," said Jake.

"I'd love to have a look around," Lucy said.

"I might be able to arrange that, I have a friend who manages the bookings for some of these cottages, I'll see if she can sort something," said Jake.

As they reached the end of the street Lucy pointed to one shop that had a queue of people lining up outside.

"Are they having a sale?" she said.

"Cornish pasties," said Jake, "the local delicacy. Come on, everyone who visits should try one."

They bought their pasties and wandered down to the harbour.

"Watch out for the sea gulls," Jake said laughing, "they're quite partial to these."

They sat and watched the boats slowly begin to float as the tide came in.

"Come back in summer and we'll hire a boat and take a ride into the bay," said Jake.

"That's sounds great but I'm not sure if I'll be back," said Lucy.

"You will, this place gets you after a while, people come back time and time again. Eventually they see it as home and, if they can, they stay," Jake said as he stared across the bay.

"We'll see," said Lucy.

"Right come on let's find those galleries," said Jake as he screwed up his paper bag and walked towards the nearest bin.

They headed back towards the town and browsed in the shops and galleries. Lucy eventually decided to buy a painting of the coast and a little cottage overlooking the sea. It was a good painting although she'd bought it more as a reminder of why she had come here. Once she was back home she could look at it and remember what she considered important to her.

"Shall we pop that in the truck and then have lunch. I have a great little restaurant lined up. It's run by a friend of mine and he serves the most amazing plate of mussels," said Jake as he took the painting and led her back to the car park.

The restaurant overlooked the harbour, Lucy was pleased as she had enjoyed watching the boats earlier, once the tide was high enough perhaps some would set off along the coast. They went through a door to the side of a little shop selling ice-cream and climbed a narrow staircase.

"Hi, Jake," said a man laying up the tables.

"Hi Finn, this is Lucy she's here on holiday so I thought I'd show her where to get the best fish and chips in town," said Jake.

"Hi, Lucy, I've reserved the best table for you," said Finn, leading them towards the window.

"Wow," said Lucy, "the views from up here are spectacular."

Jake took her coat and handed it to Finn. "I can highly recommend the mussels followed by fish and chips," he said, "and of course a bottle of Cornish wine."

"Sounds good to me," said Lucy. She usually liked to choose from the menu but she hadn't had fish and chips in ages and, if the smell from the kitchen was anything to go by, these were going to be good.

Jake looked at Lucy. "So why are you here?" asked Jake.

"I'm just having a break, it's been manic at work and I haven't been able to get away until now," said Lucy looking away from him.

"Your boss must be some taskmaster," said Jake.

"No," said Lucy. She laughed as she thought about Laura, taskmaster was the last word she would use to describe her. In fact if it hadn't been for her she probably wouldn't have survived the last few months. A real balance of sympathy and pragmatism. "She's great, and I get a bonus if we do well so it suits me to work when we're busy."

"What do you do?" Jake asked.

"I'm an estate agent, and don't make any funny remarks. Most of us are OK you know. And I always do the best for my clients," replied Lucy.

"I'm sure you do, I wouldn't dream of suggesting otherwise," Jake said laughing.

"What about you?" said Lucy.

"Well, as you know I run the café and am about to expand it into an evening restaurant," said Jake.

"I know, but you haven't been doing that for long, what did you do before that?" asked Lucy.

"I worked in London, finance. And now it's my turn to say no funny comments," he said, laughing.

"So what made you come back? I assume you're from here," Lucy said.

"Yes, born and bred. Circumstance, it was the right thing to do," said Jake, he looked out of the window to avoid Lucy's gaze.

"For who?" Lucy asked.

"For everyone I guess. Anyway I'm glad I came back. I'd forgotten what is was like to be here permanently. I don't think I'd want to leave now," said Jake, this time smiling at her.

Lucy looked at Jake, he clearly wasn't going to give anything else away and she did not want to share any of her past with him. As if on cue Finn arrived carrying two very large bowls of mussels.

"There you are Jake, Lucy," he said, "I hope it lives up to your expectations."

"Thanks," said Lucy smiling at Finn, she noted how everyone she met seemed eager to ensure she was happy.

After he had left Jake said, "Finn's not originally from here but came down seven years ago to teach surfing for the season, he helped out at this restaurant during the evenings and ended up renting the place when the owner decided to retire." Jake smiled at Lucy. "Like I said, everyone calls this place home eventually."

Lucy looked at her bowl of mussels. "You call this a starter, I'd call it lunch and dinner together," she said deciding to change the subject.

As they ate their meal they chatted about places to visit, the ever changing weather and some of the history of St Ives. Lucy occasionally glanced out of the window, she was surprised at how quickly the view changed as the tide continued to rise. Nearly all the boats in the harbour were now floating and one boat was making its way into the bay. As the sky cleared the sea changed colour from grey to blue and the paintwork on the boats appeared to brighten, as if waking up. If she had to describe the scene she'd probably use the word pretty, and yet it was more than that, even though there were few people wandering around this place was living, breathing and changing – it had a life of its own.

When the main course arrived Lucy looked at her plate of fish and chips. This was nothing like the food they dished up at her local chippie. The chips were chunky and the fish was covered in a crispy batter that crumbled at the edges when she cut into it.

"I have to admit I've never chosen fish and chips

at a restaurant before," she took a mouthful and savoured the taste, "this fish is divine."

"They only serve fresh fish here, all caught locally," said Jake as he bit into an oversized chip.

"I guess that's one of the advantages of living by the coast," said Lucy as she continued to enjoy her meal. "Will you be serving fish in your restaurant?"

"If the fishermen catch it I'll serve it," said Jake, "I want to change the menu daily based on what's available locally and what's in season."

"Local produce, I like the idea," Lucy said.

"I need to get some time to see what local producers have to offer and build my menus from there," said Jake, "we have some great foods around here, have you tried the local ice cream yet?" he asked.

"Not yet," replied Lucy, "I was waiting for the sun to shine first," she laughed.

"Well it's shining now," said Jake, "we'll have some for dessert, they make their own here."

Lucy continued with her meal and thought back to the times she had visited local markets with Mark on Saturday mornings. She enjoyed selecting ingredients and putting them together as a meal or picking up some hams and cheeses to have for breakfast. She never really thought about foods being in season, she just bought what was on sale.

"Penny for them," said Jake.

"Sorry," said Lucy looking up.

"Your thoughts, you were miles away," said Jake.

"No, just thinking about what you were saying, I think I need to think about what I buy from now on," she said hoping he wouldn't ask anything else.

"OK, it is important, but you looked decidedly

forlorn," said Jake looking directly at her.

"No," she said, "I was just thinking I need to cook more as well, and that's enough to make anyone frown," she said laughing. Not exactly the truth but she hoped she sounded convincing.

"I could teach you, or you could come here, they run workshops on a Wednesday afternoon," said Jake sounding quite excited about the whole idea.

"I think it'll take more than one afternoon for me to learn how to cook food like this, maybe I'll just eat out more," she said laughing again.

"You know that's twice you've avoided sharing why you came here," Jake said.

"I know, pretty much in the same way you've avoided sharing why you came back," Lucy said.

"It's complicated," he said.

Lucy nodded, complicated was something she could relate to.

They enjoyed the rest of their meal, Lucy finished most of the bottle of wine as Jake was driving.

"Do you want to visit the Tate now?" Jake asked.

"I'd rather have another wander around and then head back if that's OK. I can always pop back another day," said Lucy.

They followed the coastline past the harbour, on round to Porthmeor Beach and into Barnoon Cemetery. As they wandered between the headstones Jake talked about the history on the cemetery and some of the people buried there, Lucy found she was not only listening but interested in what he was saying.

"You should be a tour guide," she said.

Lucy felt totally at ease listening to Jake and was beginning to think she wouldn't mind spending more time with him. As they headed back Jake continued to entertain her with tales of ghosts, hauntings and things that go bump in the night.

"Thank-you," said Lucy, "I've had a great day."

"It was my pleasure, perhaps we could do this again before you go, you still haven't visited the Tate," Jake said.

Lucy smiled, she didn't want to get involved however she had enjoyed his company, "I'd like that," she replied.

12

Lucy woke early feeling refreshed, she wasn't sure why, maybe it was the sea air or maybe it was spending the day with Jake. She did have to admit she had enjoyed herself.

As if responding to her thoughts Jake knocked on the door and walked in carrying two cups of coffee.

"Hi," he said, "you've got me again today, and you'll probably get my services for the rest of the week as Mum is pretty tied up. I've brought your favourite coffee to make up for it," he said grinning.

"Thanks," said Lucy taking the cup off him, "you must have read my mind."

"Just one of my many talents," he said.

"It seems such a waste of your time coming to light the fire every day, why not show me how to do it, I could go home having learnt a whole new skill," said Lucy.

"I could," Jake said, "but then I'd have no excuse for popping round, and you'd miss out on your morning coffee," he said taking a sip from his own cup.

"Yes, I could see missing out on coffee as a disadvantage," she said, "but I'd still like to learn."

They both laughed. Once they'd finished their coffee they crouched in front of the woodburner. Jake showed Lucy how to check if the ashes needed removing and reminded her that they might be hot. He showed her how to use a firelighter and some kindling to get the fire going before adding a small log.

"OK, I'll give it a go tomorrow," said Lucy.

"You sure you don't want me to stop by," said

Jake.

"No, I'll be fine. Anyway I know where to find you," Lucy said.

Jake paused.

"Look I know this is a bit of a cheek but how do you fancy working at the café for a couple of evenings, Friday and Saturday. I'd pay well," he said.

"I don't think so, anyway I have no experience," said Lucy, this was a holiday to relax, not a working holiday.

"You'd be fine, you clearly like people. Look the girl who usually helps out has broken her arm and will be out of action for a few weeks and Mum won't be around. Could you just help me out this weekend. I just want to make it special," he said.

"At least that's one thing I'm good at," Lucy said.

"Well there you go, you already have all the experience needed," Jake said, he laughed hesitantly, "So will you do it?"

"OK, although I do feel I've had my arm twisted, what time do I have to be there?" Lucy said.

"Six o'clock would be great, first booking is at seven," Jake said smiling. "Shall I pick you up?"

"No thanks, I'll meet you there," Lucy said.

Jake left leaving Lucy feeling a little bemused. How did that just happen?

13

Lucy spent the next couple of days walking to the café and writing in her journal. She also enjoyed going to the local shop and selecting fresh produce to cook. Sam had been great, he had even got in a jar of her favourite coffee and Danish pastries for her breakfast. Today she had bought some fresh vegetables and made a soup. Chopping the carrots and coriander had been quite therapeutic, a blender would have made the job easier but the chunky soup was quite delicious and enough to last for a couple of days.

As she sat at the table dipping bread into her soup she read through the entries she had made in her journal.

Actions
Sell apartment.
Get apartment revalued and look at new ways to promote it in order to secure a sale.
Redecorate and furnish where necessary.
Take some photographs.
Hold an open day.

The apartment was currently being rented, the tenants were due to move out at the end of the year. It wouldn't take long to spruce the place up and turn it into something that was easy to market. She continued reading.

Buy new home.
Identify areas to live.
Research amenities.

Research commuting times and public transport.
Spend a day at each short-listed area.

When she returned home she had a lot to do, at least now she had a focus. In fact she felt quite excited by it. Lucy picked up her pen and wrote a new heading.

Hobbies and Leisure

She had her job and, until recently, had always done everything else with Mark. She wasn't really sure if she actually had the same interests as him or if she'd just chosen to do what he enjoyed. What she did know was that during the last few months she went to work, spend the evening at her parents and met up with friends once a week. She started to write a list.

Eating out with friends.
Visiting art galleries.
Painting.

She hadn't painted anything for some years now, this could be the perfect time to take it up again. In the short term she could at least start seeing her friends more often.

Lucy jumped when Jake knocked on the kitchen window, he walked on round to the back door and let himself in.

"I know it's short notice but I'm heading up to the pub, there's a band playing, some friends of mine, and I'm going along to give moral support, I thought you might enjoy it. We could have dinner if you haven't eaten," Jake said.

"That would be great, although I've already eaten," Lucy said.

"That's good as so have I, I'd have to force it down and pretend to be starving," he said laughing.

"When do you want to go, I'm not exactly dressed for a night out," Lucy said looking down at her jeans and baggy jumper.

"You look fine," he said, "it's a pretty casual affair."

She put the dishes in the sink, they'd have to wait until tomorrow, something she'd never have done with Mark or at her parents.

Lucy grabbed her coat and followed Jake out of the door.

14

The bar had a traditional feel with old wooden tables, chairs that didn't match and paintings of the local area on the walls.

"Hi, Jake," said the girl behind the bar, "what can I get you?"

As Jake was ordering Lucy noticed Sam.

"Hi," she said.

"You decided to give this place a try then," Sam said as he walked over to her.

"What would you like to drink?" Jake asked.

"A glass of red please, Merlot if you have it," Lucy said to the barmaid.

"You ready for another?" Jake said looking at Sam.

"No thanks," he said, holding up a full pint, "in fact I'll say hello and goodbye, I'm helping out here tonight and need to check everything is set up."

"Make that two glasses of Merlot, actually make that a bottle," Jake said turning back to the barmaid.

"Don't worry, I'm not driving," Jake said looking at Lucy.

Lucy realised she had no idea where Jake actually lived, not that she needed to know. Maybe he lived with his mother.

They made their way towards the tables near the make-shift stage.

"You'll enjoy this band," Jake said as he poured the wine.

"How do you know?" Lucy asked.

"Well I think they're pretty good," he said smiling.

There were ten or twelve people in the room, three of them got up and made their way towards the stage. Two men picked up guitars and the girl took hold of the mic.

"Looks like we're starting," said Jake, "these aren't the band I've brought you to see they're on third, sort of headlining," he said grinning.

The band played three tracks, two covers and one they'd written themselves. They were followed by a young man, he looked in his early twenties, playing his guitar. He played a few tracks, Lucy recognised some of them but guessed he must have written the others. She actually thought he was quite good, someone she'd happily pay to see.

"You really should come down in summer, there might be some showers and a few windy days but the weather is usually pretty good," Jake said.

"I might just do that," said Lucy as she smiled. "I'll have a chat with your mum."

"You'll need to be quick, the cottage gets booked up well before the season starts, some people come back on the same dates year after year," Jake said.

"Can't say I blame them, this place is quite special," Lucy said.

Jake refilled their glasses. "So what are you going to do when you get back to Bristol?" Jake asked.

"Probably the same as I was doing before I came down here, that's what most people do after a holiday," Lucy said.

She still wasn't ready to discuss her life with him, neither her past nor her future.

"True, I know you're an estate agent but I don't know what else you do," Jake said.

"I'm pretty tied up with work but I enjoy eating out, meeting with friends and, as you know, visiting art galleries," she said thinking about the list she recently written in her notebook, they were the things she enjoyed doing even if she didn't actually do them.

"I need to take you to the Tate before you leave, when would you like to go?" Jake asked.

The final band came on saving Lucy from having to answer. The music was lively and Lucy found herself tapping to the beat. She made a mental note that she needed to get out and see some local bands when she got back to Bristol, another item to add to her list.

"Come on, let's check out the weather," Lucy said as she finished the last of her wine and put on her coat.

Jake walked her back to the cottage and said goodbye at the gate. As Lucy made herself a coffee she felt a twinge of regret that she hadn't offered one to Jake.

15

The first week had flown by, Lucy had spent her days enjoying the Cornish coastline and, when it wasn't raining, taking her notebook onto the dunes. So far she had a short list of things to do when she returned home. She hadn't written anything about relationships, when she had arrived they were very much off the agenda, now she felt that maybe, at some point, she did want a future which included a partner.

As the evening approached Lucy thought it a good idea to find something suitable to wear for her first night working at the café. She laid out three outfits on the bed - jeans and t-shirt, blue skirt and cream sweater, cream slacks and black fitted top. She hadn't exactly packed with work in mind. She'd been to the café during the day and it all seemed pretty casual but maybe Jake wanted a smarter look for the evening. Blue skirt it was then, smart but not over the top. She swept her hair back off her face and secured it in a loose pony tail, finally she applied just a little make-up.

"You'll have to do," she said aloud as she looked in the mirror.

Lucy set off in plenty of time, she might be doing Jake a favour but she didn't like being late. In a way she was quite looking forward to this evening, she had never actually worked in a café or restaurant before and, even though she was a little nervous about making a mistake or spilling the soup, she liked the idea of meeting people. Good job she'd found the torch, she could see the lights of the houses and pub ahead but the lane was dark, really dark.

"Thanks for coming," Jake said as Lucy walked

into the café, "we're not that busy, well we're full actually but that isn't too busy as we can only seat sixteen people. There's just the two of us, you take orders and bring them to me. I'll cook and shout you when the food is ready. At the moment we don't sell alcohol though guests can bring their own. We just put glasses on the table and a jug of water," Jake continued without pausing for breath.

"Right, I think, can we start again from the beginning," said Lucy feeling a little nervous that Jake seemed to think she knew what she was doing.

Jake laughed.

"Sorry, I'm just nervous because this is our opening night," he said, "we have to get the tables ready so I'll talk you through the menu while we set up."

"You mean you haven't actually done this before?" Lucy said.

"Not the evening meals, but don't worry, it'll be fine. There's no-one to wash up so just stack everything on the side and I'll do it later. Luckily I've got plenty of plates, bought a job lot," Jake said.

Lucy picked up the tray of cutlery and started to lay the tables according to the plan Jake had given her. Four tables for two, and two tables for four. At least they were arriving throughout the evening which should give her time to learn the ropes.

Lucy placed the glasses on the table, put jugs of water in the fridge and checked the ice supply.

"You know what you need," she said turning to Jake, "flowers and those little glass holders with tea lights."

"That's not a bad idea, perhaps we could get some next week," Jake said.

"Count me out, this is a one off. I'm already

nervous and the customers haven't even arrived yet," Lucy said as she held out a shaking hand to show Jake.

Right on cue two people walked through the door, Sam from the shop and a young woman.

"Hi Jake, are we OK to come in," said Sam.

"Of course" Jake said, "You're our first customers."

"Lucy, this is Sam and Jenny, Sam you know and I went to school with Jenny although she was in the younger class," said Jake.

"Hello, can I take your coats, and I'll open the wine for you," she said as she noticed Sam was holding a bottle of white.

Jake smiled, and made his way to the kitchen leaving Lucy to seat the couple.

Ten minutes later Lucy went into the kitchen

"Two smoked salmon, one sea bass and one steak, medium rare," she said handing Jake the order.

"Have you done this before?" Jake said.

"No but I've seen it on the telly," Lucy said.

"I'll shout when the starters are ready," Jake said.

"Yes, chef," Lucy said grinning.

As Lucy left the kitchen four people arrived. She greeted them and gave out the menus.

"Salmon's ready," called Jake.

Lucy collected the starters and put them in front of Sam and Jenny.

"Enjoy," she said.

She was actually quite enjoying herself.

Soon all the guests had arrived and were enjoying their meals.

Sixteen people did not sound a lot but with seating guests, taking orders, collecting food from the kitchen, clearing tables, serving wine and going back to take dessert orders, Lucy was exhausted. She did manage to stay on top of things – just.

After the last dessert had been served Jake came out of the kitchen to chat with his customers. He looked at Lucy, "The sooner I get someone to wash up the better, I wasn't worried about the crockery but the kitchen looks like a bomb's hit, perhaps if I just go home the elves will come and tidy up."

Lucy grinned, "Well I'm going to add to it, there's plenty more to clear," she said, "and I think it's the elves night off."

"Oh well," could be a busy morning.

"You can't leave it until morning, when everyone's finished I'll give you a hand," Lucy said.

"You don't have to do that," Jake said.

"I know, but since I agreed to help I need to make sure the job is finished properly," she said.

After they had said goodbye to the last of the guests Lucy led Jake into the kitchen.

"I'll wash, you dry," said Lucy.

"We make quite a team don't we," said Jake as he picked up a clean tea towel.

Lucy looked at him and grinned. "Just for one weekend," she said.

16

It was another hour before they'd finished cleaning the kitchen. Jake handed Lucy her coat and locked up behind them.

"Mum's borrowed the truck so I'll walk you back and then go and pick it up," Jake said.

"There's no need, it's not far," Lucy said.

"Do you really think I'd let you walk back on your own, especially after all you've done tonight. And thank-you again. You really made a difference you know, the customers loved you. One even asked when you were working again," Jake said.

"I'm sure they'll love your new waitress, or waiter, just as much, do you have anyone yet?" Lucy asked.

"Not yet, I've asked around, hopefully I'll get someone soon though," Jake replied. "We can cut across the dunes here and re-join the lane further up, we can follow the path easily enough in this light."

Lucy looked at the sky. "I don't think I've seen so many stars, it's stunning," she said.

"Not much light pollution around here, you've probably noticed there aren't even street lights once you leave the main road," Jake said.

Lucy pulled her coat a little tighter around her, it might be dry, but the wind had picked up, somehow it cut right through her.

"I'm sorry, I should have called you a taxi," Jake said.

"Don't be daft, it's not far and I'm enjoying the walk. I'll bring an extra jumper next time," she said.

"Next time, that's sounds promising," Jake said.

Lucy laughed. "Well I did say I'd do tomorrow as well," she said.

"I know but I thought you might hate it and refuse," Jake said.

"I didn't hate it, I like working with people. Though I wouldn't say washing up that many dishes was high on my things to do before I'm forty list," she said laughing.

Almost too soon for Lucy's liking they reached the cottage.

"Would you like to come in for a coffee?" Lucy asked as she took the key out of her bag.

"I'd like to but I won't, you look exhausted. Same time tomorrow?" Jake said.

"See you there," she replied. She felt a little disappointed that Jake wasn't staying.

There was still a slight glow in the woodburner. Jake might have thought she was tired but there was no way she could sleep just yet. Lucy poured herself a glass of wine and picked up the book she'd started to read. It was another hour before she made her way to bed.

17

Lucy spent Saturday afternoon relaxing in the bath and reading her novel. She felt much calmer about working that evening and only took a few minutes to get ready, she dressed a little more casually, mainly because of her limited wardrobe. Lucy was looking forward to her second night at the café as she had genuinely enjoyed working there - the customers were delightful and obviously appreciated the food Jake cooked. Even though it was only the two of them they had made worked well together ensuring everyone had an enjoyable evening.

As she walked down the lane. Lucy heard the truck before she saw it, she stepped to the side and waved her torch a little as Jake's Toyota came into view. He pulled alongside her and wound down the window.

"Hi," he said grinning, "thought you might appreciate my door to door service."

"Thanks," said Lucy "but you didn't have to, I enjoy the walk." She smiled surprised at how pleased she was to see him.

"I was going this way anyway so thought I ought to stop," Jake said.

"No you weren't, this road doesn't go anywhere," she said as she walked around the truck and opened the passenger door.

Jake grabbed some papers from the front seat and threw them into the back. "OK, you found me out, I just wanted to make sure you got there safe and sound. I don't fancy cooking and serving tonight," he said.

"I hope those weren't important," said Lucy as she climbed into the passenger seat.

"No, just some ideas for a menu for a party next week," he said.

"Can I see?" Lucy asked.

"Maybe, actually I'd welcome your thoughts. We'll take a look after we've finished serving tonight," Jake said. "I really do appreciate you helping me out like this, I know this is supposed to be a holiday for you," Jake said.

"To be honest I'm actually quite enjoying it, perhaps I've found my true calling," Lucy said smiling at Jake.

"Well I was wondering, since you are enjoying it so much, do you think you could do next Friday. I've got a 40th birthday party booked in, they're taking over the whole restaurant, and I want it to go well. The customers really like you," Jake said grinning.

"Thanks, I think, yes next Friday's fine, after that I am off home though," said Lucy.

"I'll pay you well," Jake said.

"You can pay me by taking me out for the day. I've been here a week and only managed to explore the local area. I wouldn't mind finding out a bit more about the place," said Lucy.

"So you're asking me to take you on a date," Jake said laughing, "where do you want to go?"

"Surprise me," she said, "and it's not a date."

"Whatever you say," he said as he looked at Lucy and grinned, "I'll give it some thought and make it really special."

"Not too special, just somewhere interesting," she said.

Jake pulled up the narrow lane that ran along the dunes and parked behind the café.

"OK, interesting it is," Jake said.

"I've a feeling I might just regret asking," Lucy said.

18

Lucy thoroughly enjoyed the evening at the restaurant, the customers were complimentary of the food and the service. Every table left a good tip. She must remember to say thank-you a bit more when she was eating out, and she could probably tip a bit better. She hadn't really thought about it until now but giving a tip wasn't really about the money, it was more about telling someone you appreciated their efforts.

"That's us done then," said Jake as he switched off the kitchen lights.

"Yes, it's been fun, I'll almost miss this when I go home," said Lucy.

"I'll run you home, and no arguing this time," said Jake.

"OK, but only if you stop for coffee, I'm still buzzing from tonight and will never get to sleep," she said.

"And you think coffee will help?" said Jake.

"We could try decaf," she said.

"OK, you've twisted my arm," Jake said.

"Sounds painful," said Lucy laughing.

****

Back in the cottage Lucy went into the kitchen whilst Jake put a log on the fire, it wasn't long before a small flame started to flicker around its base.

"That'll soon catch," he said," just close the vent when you go to bed and it'll just burn away slowly."

"Will do," Lucy called back.

Rather than make coffee she opened a bottle of Merlot. It hadn't had chance to breath but then she hadn't exactly planned this night cap. Well if she was going to take control of her life surely that included deciding who she invited to stay. She took a deep breath and carried the glasses of wine into the sitting room.

"I believe you like Merlot," she said.

"You do realise that if I drink this I won't be able to drive home," Jake said as he took the glass from Lucy.

"I was rather banking on it," she replied not daring to look him in the eyes.

19

Lucy opened her eyes as the smell of frying bacon wafted up the stairs. She looked at the time on her mobile – nine-twenty. The smell was too good to resist so she put on her robe and went downstairs.

"Good morning," said Jake.

"Where did you get those from," said Lucy pointing to the box of eggs, "there were none in the fridge?"

"I popped down to the shop while you were sleeping," said Jake.

"It's Sunday, they can't be open yet," Lucy said.

"It's nearly nine-thirty you know, but you're right, just as well I know Sam, he was happy, well almost, to get out of bed and serve me," Jake said laughing. "I've made you a coffee and lit the fire."

Jake put the eggs and bacon onto two plates and cut some bread from the loaf he'd found in the bread bin.

"Eat up I've got a busy day planned for you," Jake said.

Lucy noticed the mischievous look in his eyes.

"And what might we be doing, something in the warm I hope," she said.

"Well you said you wanted to get to know the place better so I thought I'd show you some sites worth seeing. A little bit of history," Jake said.

As they were enjoying breakfast there was a knock on the door.

"Come on in Mum," shouted Jake.

"Hi Annie," said Lucy blushing as she realised Annie knew Jake had stayed overnight.

Annie had brought a picnic packed into a rucksack. "I'm not sure what you like so I've packed a selection of sandwiches and cake. I've put in a flask of hot chocolate as well as coffee, I think you're might need it, you are brave," she said.

"What do you mean brave, and why the picnic?" Lucy asked.

Annie looked at Jake. "Are you sure this is a good idea at this time of year," she said.

"It'll be fine, and fun, and a great way to see what Cornwall has to offer," Jake said.

"Come on Jake, tell me what you're up to, if its wild swimming I may never speak to you again," Lucy said.

"No we're not going into the water though we might get wet looking at the forecast," Jake said. "OK, time to get dressed and set off. You need to wrap up warm."

"This is sounding better by the minute," Lucy said.

"I've a couple of windproof jackets in the truck, we'll probably need those even if it doesn't rain," said Jake laughing.

"What exactly are we doing? It sound very outside," Lucy asked.

"You'll see," said Jake.

Lucy got into the truck beside Jake. They headed along the coast road for about four miles. Every now and again she could see the steep cliffs that dropped away to the sea. The sun was shining however Lucy had come to realise this could be deceiving. As they headed down a steep hill she caught a glimpse of a beach, the sea looked ominous as wave after wave crashed against the shore.

"I hope we're not going in there," she said, "as much as I like swimming I prefer warm water with a gentle swell."

Jake laughed. "What you don't fancy the surf today," he said.

"Not a chance," she said.

"Shame, I thought you'd enjoy it. Oh well plan b it is then," said Jake still grinning.

Jake swung the car away from the beach and started to head uphill. A short distance away he pulled into a farm drive, a woman was stood in the doorway of the barn holding two bikes.

"You have got to be kidding," Lucy said.

"Other than going by boat, which I thought might be stretching things a bit too far, this has got to be one of the best ways to see at least some of the area," Jake said.

Jake parked the truck in the yard and handed a jacket to Lucy.

"You can ride a bike?" Jake asked.

"Yes, I'm not keen on the traffic though," Lucy said.

"Don't worry we won't meet much in the way of traffic," Jake said.

"I'm not sure if that sounds better or worse," she said.

"Are you ready?" he said as they collected the bikes.

"As I'll ever be," Lucy replied.

Lucy pushed her bike down the steep drive, Jake laughed as he free-wheeled, braked hard at the end, crossed the road and waited on the cycle path.

"We've got all day so we can go at the pace you're happy with," Jake said.

They set off together and took a right down a quiet lane, a few minutes later they were on a narrow track. The route Jake had chosen brought them out onto a main road however the cycle track kept them away from the traffic.

"It is pretty but I haven't seen anything that interesting yet," Lucy said.

"You will," Jake replied.

After about half an hour they were again off-road. This time it was a little more challenging - mud, puddles and some significantly steep hills. The path took them through a wooded area before opening out into a quarry.

"Look up there," Jake said pointing to the right.

"Wow," said Lucy as she looked at what looked like the ruins of a building, "what's that?"

"One of the old mines. We'll see a few on this route," Jake said as he cycled up the bank to explore the remains of the mine.

"How old of these buildings?" Lucy asked as she followed him.

"Nineteenth century, though this area was being mined long before that. Mining used to be big business here, in fact much of the path we are cycling used to be a railway line, look closely and you can even see some of the old sleepers," he said.

They free-wheeled their bikes back down the hill and onto the track. Mark continued to point out the mine shafts and entertained her with tales of hard working miners and rich mine owners.

"You seem know a lot about this place," Lucy said. "Do you come here often?" she asked, laughing.

"I used to," he said, "when I was younger. I'd actually forgotten how beautiful it was, even in November." He paused for a moment and looked around. "A few more miles and we'll stop at a café, I know we've got a picnic but I think some hot food wouldn't go amiss."

"Jake," Lucy said.

"Yes," he said.

"What made you leave here?" Lucy asked.

"Same as most people I guess, went off to uni and just never came back. Got a job, was earning good money and having plenty of fun," Jake said.

"So what made you come back?" she said.

Jake looked ahead. "It was just the right time. Anyway what about you. You don't seem like the type of girl who'd choose Cornwall for a winter holiday," he said.

"And what type of girl is that?" Lucy said.

"Oh I don't know, smart, sophisticated, a city lover," he replied.

"That almost sounds like a compliment," Lucy said avoiding the question.

"So, what brought you down here at this time of year?" he asked again.

"I just needed so thinking time, maybe make some decisions," she replied.

"Sounds like a man was involved," he said.

"You sound like your mum," Lucy said.

Determined not to answer any more questions Lucy said, "tell me about this party next weekend, it seems important to you."

"It's for some friends of mine, they've been through a lot lately and I want to make is special," he said with a touch of sadness in his voice.

"That's very thoughtful, you sound like someone who's worth having as a friend," she said.

"I am," Jake grinned.

"What are you doing tomorrow?" Lucy asked.

"I've got to pop out after I've finished at the coffee shop," he said.

"Anything I can help you with," she said.

"Boring stuff, just some business. Drop by the

café on Tuesday and we can discuss plans for the party," Jake grinned.

"Maybe I will," said Lucy feeling a little disappointed.

"Come on, let's finish this bike ride there's more to see," Jake said.

After stopping at the café they rode on through a valley until they came to a viaduct with some tall pillars standing beside it.

"Now this was designed by someone you would definitely have heard of," Jake said, pointing to the pillars.

Lucy looked at him quizzically.

"Isambard Kingdom Brunel, did a lot of work in your neck of the woods I believe," Jake said.

Lucy smiled. "I believe he did," she said.

"Are you staying for dinner?" Lucy asked as they turned back.

"I can't, I have to take Mum into Truro," he said.

"On a Sunday evening," Lucy said.

"She's visiting a relative and prefers not to drive back," he said.

"A dutiful son as well as a good friend. Do you have any faults?" Lucy asked.

"Many, though hopefully none you'll hear about, I've sworn everyone to secrecy," he said.

They both laughed.

20

Lucy had all of Monday to herself, she should have been looking forward to it and yet she found herself wishing she was meeting Jake. Well she wasn't going to stalk him so the café was out of bounds. She flicked through some of the leaflets Annie had left and decided to visit Truro, it seemed an interesting city and wasn't that far away if the map was anything to go by. Lucy checked she had her camera in her bag and set off, she realised this was the first time she'd driven her car since she'd been here. Luckily it started first time.

She was quite surprised at just how long it took her to drive to the city, the map indicated it was about twenty miles away, that might be true but it took double the time she expected.

Lucy decided to visit the cathedral first, as she approached the impressive building she looked up at its spires and took a several photographs. Once inside she could truly appreciate the scale and detail of the stained glass windows, each telling their own tale. The cathedral provided an excellent opportunity to practise her photography skills. Lucy choose her subjects carefully picking out different carvings, inscriptions and windows, she took her time to frame each one and adjust her camera until she was happy with the picture. It was over an hour before she was ready to leave. Before she left she visited the cathedral shop and bought an advent calendar, something she hadn't had since she was a child.

She wandered around the streets for a while enjoying using her camera for pleasure. Lucy photographed many of the buildings, both old and new, trying to capture the character and history of the place.

It was nearly two o'clock before she felt hungry, she found a little tea room situated above a vintage shop and made her way up the stairs.

"Table for one?" the waitress asked.

"Yes please," she said.

"Follow me, would you like a window seat?" the waitress asked.

"Yes please," she said again.

Lucy ordered a cappuccino, and cranberry and brie on toast, posh cheese on toast she thought to herself. As she sipped her coffee she took out her notebook and started to write.

Relationships (men)
It doesn't seem that long since Mark left and I didn't think that I could trust anyone else again – maybe I can't. And yet being with Jake does make me think that maybe I was just unlucky, seems a bit flippant to say that but I do enjoy Jake's company and he does seem genuine. Of course I'm leaving soon so am unlikely to see him again but maybe there are other Jakes out there and, in time, I'll meet one. On the other hand maybe we could stay in touch, after all what's four hours between friends, it's not like he's living in another country. Of course he may not want to stay in touch, perhaps it's easy for him to be friendly when he knows I'm leaving and yet…

Lucy paused, she had intended to think about whether she wanted another man in her life, consider how she could trust again and also decide if she wanted a long term relationship. She found that all she could think about was Jake. So much for not falling for the waiter. Perhaps she needed a different question – did she want Jake? Did he want her? If yes then how could they make this work? She started to write again.

Is Jake boyfriend material?

She laughed as she reread the words, she sounded like a teenager.

If I have another relationship what do I want? Loyalty, honesty, commitment, a family.

She smiled, she was unlikely to have this conversation with Jake, she'd only known him a week, now was not the right time to broach the question of how many children they should have.

Am I ready for a new relationship? Am I ready for Jake?

These were not questions she could answer today or even this week. She did however feel that maybe she was ready to consider seeing someone new. Maybe she was ready to allow someone else into her life and perhaps even share parts of it with them. Lucy put her pen down as the waitress brought across her lunch.

The cheese on toast wasn't quite what she'd expected - thick slices of fresh bread coated with cranberries and covered in brie. It looked incredible.

Lucy glanced out of the window, she looked down and was surprised to see Jake across the road from her. She waved but he didn't look up, probably a good thing. Lucy wondered briefly what he was doing here, he hadn't actually said he was working at the café all day but he'd definitely given her that impression. Lucy noticed a woman running behind him, she must have called out because Jake stopped and turned around. He smiled and said something then held out his arms and hugged her. Not a quick *hello* type of hug, more of a *I know you very well and don't want to let you go* type of hug. They were obviously pleased to see each other.

Lucy looked away, she felt the tears form in the corner of her eyes. How could she have been such a fool? Would she ever learn?

"Are you OK," the waitress asked as she came to collect her plate.

Lucy realised tears had started to roll down her cheeks, "yes, I'm fine. It's just been a difficult day," she said.

Lucy paid her bill and walked back to her car. To top it off it had started to rain and she hadn't brought her umbrella.

21

The sound of the rain lashing against the window made Lucy feel cold, she put another log on the woodburner and curled up on the sofa with her book. When she heard a knock on the door she decided not to answer it, if it was Annie she would let herself in, if it was Jake – well he could just go away. Whoever was at the door didn't go away and had started banging harder, Lucy put her book down and opened the door ready to share a few choice words with Jake.

"Mark, what are you doing here?" Lucy said, she couldn't hide her surprise as he was the last person she expected to see.

"Hi," said Mark, a little sheepishly. "I know you're going to tell me to leave but how about one coffee."

"Not a chance, and how did you find me?" she said.

"I had to come down here for work, I couldn't find the location and was using my phone's locator app when you popped up only a few minutes away from my client. You obviously haven't deleted me," Mark said with a hint of a smile.

"That wasn't top of my to do list, in fact I haven't given you any thought in ages," she said knowing that this wasn't exactly true.

"Well I think it must be fate," he said.

"You don't believe in fate," she said still standing in the doorway.

"Look I wanted to catch up with you in the next few days so this seemed an opportune moment. The estate agent has been in contact, the couple who are renting our apartment want to extend for another six months. I know we said we would sell but I think we should reconsider," Mark said.

"I really want to sell, I intend to put a deposit down a new place pretty soon," Lucy said.

"Prices are still rising and we could make extra money if we wait another six months or even a year. It makes great financial sense. Perhaps you could stay with your parents a little longer, they have plenty of room," he said.

"I plan to move out after Christmas," Lucy said.

"Rent then, I am sure that you will have made more from our property in six months than you will have paid out in rent, after all you don't need a huge place. It would give you a bigger deposit," Mark said.

"Let me think about it," Lucy said.

"You can see it makes sense," Mark said.

"I said let me think about it," she said determined not to be pushed into something by Mark even if it was a good idea.

"OK but I need to know this week so the tenants can renew," Mark said.

"Don't push it," Lucy said.

"Look, you have every right to be angry with me but I made a mistake, I'm truly sorry," he said.

"You're sorry, what on earth is that meant to mean," she said, she could feel her anger rise.

"I treated to appallingly, I know," he said.

"Just go back home, I'll call when I've thought about the apartment," she said.

"OK, but one coffee please, it's a long drive back," he said.

Lucy looked at him, one coffee wouldn't hurt.

"One coffee, and then you go, I have no desire to reminisce over old times," she said.

She directed him into the kitchen, she didn't want him to get too comfortable.

"Well this is cosy," said Mark as he sat down at the little kitchen table.

"I like it," she replied, "it might be a holiday cottage but I'd love somewhere like this."

"Wow, you've certainly changed, what happened to the apartment living, must have plenty of space Lucy," Mark said.

"I think I can say she is well and truly in the past," Lucy replied.

"I get what you mean about this place, it might be small but it has character, and it seems to have everything you need," Mark said.

"Don't pretend you like it, I really can't imagine you anywhere else except right in the centre of the city," Lucy said.

"You know me so well," Mark said grinning.

"Obviously I didn't know you at all," Lucy said, feeling a little calmer.

"Oh you did, I know I made a massive mistake and there's no going back from that but you always knew me better than anyone else. I know there are no excuses but I think I had a bit of a mid-life crisis," Mark said.

"You're 34, that was not a mid-life crisis," Lucy said, almost laughing, it didn't take long for her to start to mellow, she always found it easy to laugh with Mark.

"We're no longer together you know," Mark said.

"Like I said I haven't been keeping tabs on you," Lucy said.

Mark picked up his coffee and wandered into the sitting room.

"It didn't take me long to realise I'd got it all wrong, I think Laura knew that too," he said.

"Why would you think I'd even care," she said, although she would like to know what had happened.

"I know we're never going to get back together but I did think that maybe we could be…" he said.

"Be what – friends, I don't think so," she said, laughing.

"Perhaps civil, we've still got the apartment so we'll need to speak sometimes," he said.

"As long as you understand the ground rules I am happy to have a conversation with you," Lucy said.

"And the ground rules are?" Mark asked.

"I'll write you a list," she said with half a smile on her face.

"I know you don't want to reminisce but this cottage is similar to the one we rented in Greece," said Mark.

"In what way?" she asked.

"That cosy feel, small but complete," said Mark.

"I know what you mean, I hadn't thought about it but yes, you're right," Lucy said.

Before Lucy new it they were talking about old times, friends they'd shared and places they'd visited.

"It's ten thirty already," Mark said, "I'd better find a hotel, it's too late to drive back tonight."

"You'll find a few hotels in here," Lucy said as she handed him the information pack.

Mark tried the number on the first leaflet.

"I can't get a signal," he said, "can I use your phone?"

Lucy looked at her screen as she handed her phone to Mark, "I don't think you'll have much luck with mine," she said, "look, the bed's made up in the spare room, you can stay tonight but I want you gone first thing in the morning."

Mark grinned, "Thanks," he said, "you won't even know I'm here. I've got a bottle of wine in the car, shall I get it?"

Lucy shrugged. "You might as well," she said, "I could do with a glass."

22

For the second time in a week Lucy woke to the smell of bacon, she had never known Mark cook breakfast before. She reached down beside the bed trying to find her handbag, now seemed like a good time to write in her notebook. Yes she still wanted changes to her life but maybe having Mark as a friend was a possibility. She didn't want to rekindle any old flames but perhaps they could be a little more than just civil, after all, he was right, they had enjoyed some great times together. She must have left her bag downstairs, she'd have to make some notes later.

As Lucy made her way downstairs she could hear Mark cursing, obviously not used to working in such a small space. She briefly wondered what his new place was like and where it was, she presumed he'd been the one to move out from Laura's apartment.

"Enjoy your lie in," said Mark as he handed her a cappuccino from the shop up the road.

"I'd like to remind you I'm on holiday and this is my new getting up time," said Lucy. She sat to the little table, "how did you know I enjoyed this coffee?"

"Lucky guess," he said, "I was hoping we could make an early start, I've got plans for us, eat up," he continued as he placed a plate of bacon butties on the table and sat down opposite her.

"I thought you were off first thing," she said as she bit into her sandwich.

"I was but, as a way of saying thank-you I've book us into a spa for the day, lunch included. It might be a little more enjoyable than putting up with this weather," said Mark.

"What are you on about, the sun's shining, it's a great day for a walk along the beach." Lucy replied.

"You might be right but as it's all paid for we'd better stick with the plan, anyway it'll give us chance to talk," he said.

Lucy continued to eat her butty, she liked the idea of the spa but if there were going to get on she would need to have a chat with Mark about booking things before asking her what she'd like to do.

Mark's phone began to buzz, he looked at the screen and sighed. "Sorry but I've got to take this, work," he said, "I'll go outside as I'll get a better signal." He hit the accept button and walked out into the back yard.

Lucy finished her breakfast and collected the wood basket from the sitting room, she enjoyed lighting the fire in the mornings. As she filled her basket from the wood store she could hear Mark on the phone, she had heard enough of his work calls to have no interest in this one. His boss expected him to be available twenty-four seven and to drop everything when he called. This conversation seemed no different.

"You know I'm working," she heard him say.

"I'll try and get back tomorrow," he continued. Typical of his boss, sending him down here to work and expecting him to be back in Bristol, this took multi-tasking to a whole new level.

"Of course I'd rather be back there with you," Mark said, a little more quietly this time.

Lucy put the basket down, this did not sound like work.

"Yes I know, but what can I do. If I've any chance of getting that promotion I need to secure this client," Mark said. "I'll see what I can do, if I can get everything tied up down here I might be able to get back tonight."

There was a brief pause.

"I love you too," he said.

Lucy picked up the basket of wood, carried it into the sitting room and started to build up the fire.

"Sorry about that," said Mark as he walked into the sitting room still holding his phone. "You know what they're like."

"I know," said Lucy.

"Look I think I'll have to head back to Bristol this afternoon, we can still go to the spa, though it might be best if we take separate cars to save me doubling back," said Mark.

Lucy looked at him. "I think it best if you leave now," she said.

"Work might be important but today you come first," he said smiling at her, "come on, let's go and enjoy ourselves and have that talk."

"This is the talk Mark, I overheard you on the phone. You are leaving right now," she said sounding totally calm. "And in answer to your question yesterday, we are selling the apartment as soon as I get back to Bristol."

Mark picked up his car keys and collected his bag. He didn't say another word as he left the cottage.

Only when Lucy could no longer hear the sound of his car did she start to cry. Why did she think she could trust him? She noticed her handbag beside the settee, she must have left it there last night. She took out her notebook and started to write.

Absolutely no serious or long term relationships. Focus on work and build up a career or business.

She looked at the word business, she'd given it some thought over the last few days but nothing had come to mind. Since she would be able to throw herself into it without any distractions now would be an excellent time to take the plunge. She started to write in her notebook again

Skills – estate agent, customer service, making dreams come true.

That was what she was really good at, making other people's dreams come true. Pity she struggled so much with her own. Did she even know what her dreams were anymore? She picked up her pen again.

What are my dreams?

She had absolutely no idea.

23

Lucy woke late the next morning, probably a result of the bottle of wine she'd consumed. After a quick breakfast she put on her coat and set off on a walk. A good bout of sea air should clear her head. She'd only made it as far as the driveway when Jake pulled his truck alongside her. She had no choice but to stop as he wound down the window.

"Hi," he said, there was a slight tone of accusation in his voice, "I called by yesterday to bring your morning coffee, Mark made it clear that you needed your rest, I'm guessing that's the boyfriend you don't want to talk about."

Lucy thought about the coffee Mark had given her, he hadn't gone to the shop at all.

"Well I guess we both have things we don't want to share," she said.

"I have no idea what you're talking about but I get the distinct feeling you are avoiding me," he said, "I thought we were getting along just fine."

"So did I," she said, "my friends are quite entitled to secrets but I'd rather they didn't lie to me," she said.

"I'm still confused, but whatever it is I'm sorry. Look I called by to check about Friday night," he said, "I didn't come here to argue, or upset you. But I really would be grateful if you could still help out. This is a special party and I genuinely mean it when I say you are fantastic with the customers. I've sorted the menu and was just checking you can make it for five thirty."

Lucy really didn't want to work with Jake again however she'd made a commitment and she didn't want to be the one to spoil the party.

"I'll be there," she said.

24

One more night at the cottage and then Lucy would be driving back to Bristol. This holiday hadn't exactly turned out the way she planned but maybe it was what she needed. All she had to do was get through tonight and then she could start building a new life for herself.

When she arrived at the café Annie was there with Jake. They had clearly been working hard. The tables had been laid out in a U shape and balloons tied to each chair.

"Hi Lucy," said Annie, "Jake said you're quite a star here."

"Thank-you, but this is my last shift, I'm going back home tomorrow," she said.

"It's a shame you can't stay longer, you've been such a good guest, I feel I ought to give you a refund," said Annie, laughing.

"You already gave me a good discount, and the cottage was great. Just the kind of change I needed," Lucy said.

"Did I see a young man there the other day?" Annie asked.

Lucy felt her body stiffen.

"Sorry Lucy, I didn't mean to upset you," Annie said.

"No, it's me, I don't seem to be able to make the right choices when it comes to men," she relaxed a little and laughed. "Ah well, all behind me now. A fresh start as soon as I get back. Anyway what do you want me to do?"

"What you do best, look after the customers. This party is quite special so I want to make sure Jake can join them as soon as possible," Annie said.

"Are they friends of Jake's?" Lucy asked.

Annie looked surprised

"I guess you could say that, has he not told you about the party," Annie said.

"Not much, just that it's a 40th birthday," Lucy said.

The door opened and the first guests arrived, Lucy recognised Sam and a couple of other people she had seen at the pub. Jake had done a seating plan so everyone knew where to go. Within twenty minutes most of the guests had sat down, Lucy assumed the four remaining seats were for the guests of honour.

Lucy and Annie were serving wine when the door opened again. Lucy recognised the woman immediately, she'd only seen her once before – in Truro with her arms wrapped around Jake.

"Is Jake in the kitchen," the woman called across to Annie as she walked across the room without waiting for a reply. Moments later she returned with Jake on her arm. Lucy watched them as they headed outside together.

Annie looks across at Lucy smiling and with a hint of pride on her face. "I've got two fantastic sons," she said, "and Sarah, who's the nearest thing I have to a daughter."

Before Lucy could ask her what she meant the door opened again, the woman, presumably Sarah, held the door as two young girls followed her in and stood beside her.

Still holding the door Sarah started a countdown. "Three, two, one," she shouted.

Every cheered as Jake walked in pushing a slightly older version of himself in a wheelchair.

"Surprise," they all shouted.

Lucy looked back at Annie and noticed she had tears in her eyes.

Annie smiled at her. "It's been hard this last year, after Ben's accident," she said, "Jake was great and came home straight away, his girlfriend didn't follow him though. As far as I'm concerned she wasn't much of a girlfriend."

Lucy tried to make sense of it all.

"He's helped me with the cottage and made sure Sarah and the kids were fine," Annie said. "Things are beginning to look better now, Ben's back home even if he has to make regular trips to the hospital."

"I'm sorry, Jake never mentioned it," Lucy said.

"He won't talk about it, he just gets on and does what has to be done. I guess it's his way of coping. With a bit of luck we can all start looking to the future now," Annie said.

The party went well, Jake had prepared most of the food in advance so he was able to keep popping out of the kitchen and chat to his friends and family. It was well after midnight before everyone had left.

"You can always tell a good party by the amount of party poppers," Lucy said to Annie, "I'll help clean up before I go."

"No you won't," said Jake as he handed Lucy and Annie a glass of wine, "this time it really can wait until the morning."

"Well here's to us," said Annie, "a job well done."

"I'll walk you back after this," said Jake.

"There's no need," said Lucy.

"You must've realised by now that I'm not going to let you walk back by yourself, anyway I'm going your way, I'm staying at Mum's tonight," Jake said.

"Look I'm sorry Jake, I know I've been off with

you but Mark turned up out of the blue and it threw me for a while," she said knowing that this was only partly true.

Jake looked at her. "Like you said we all have things we don't want to share," he said, "look there's something I'd like to ask you. Don't answer straight away but give it some thought."

"Sounds intriguing," said Lucy.

"Come and work for me, here at the café. You could rent the cottage for a while – I think I can negotiate a good rate," he said smiling as he looked at Annie. "We'd be a great team, we are a great team."

"I don't need to think about it," Lucy replied, "the answers no."

Jake looked a little taken aback, "I thought you enjoyed working here, and I know you have lots of ideas that could really put this place on the map."

"I did, or rather I do enjoy working here, I just don't want to work for you," she said.

"Am I that bad a boss," he said laughing a little nervously.

"No, I just don't want to work for anyone," Lucy said. She stood quietly for a few moments, if she was going to change her life maybe she did need to take a risk and perhaps now was as good a time as any.

"Can I make you a counter offer," she said looking directly at Jake.

"I guess so," he said.

"Let me buy into the business," she said, "I won't work for you but I will work with you."

Lucy breathed out, she had no idea how she was going to make this work. She would get some money from the sale of the apartment and might be able to take out a loan. Of course she'd have to give notice and tell her parents she was moving away.

"I've always done things on my own, made all the decisions," Jake said.

"Your call," said Lucy with a new found confidence, "you don't need to answer straightaway, take some time to think about it."

It was Jake's turn to look at her quietly for a few moments.

"No," he said, "I mean yes, what I actually mean is no I don't need time to think about it and yes I'd like you to accept your offer."

Lucy held out her hand. "Partners," she said.

Jake took her hand and shook it. "Partners," he said.

****

Lucy loaded her suitcases into her car, started the engine and sat looking at the cottage. She took her notebook from the glove compartment and made one final entry.

Home – move to Cornwall.
Business – run a café.
Relationships – maybe, just maybe.

The End

Also by Lily Wells

The Vintage Tea Room
end of an era and new beginnings

Ellie is about to change her life. As spring arrives in the Cotswold town of Cirencester she decides it's time to sell the tea room she's been running for more than twenty years. Ellie wants to spend more time doing some of the things she enjoys and, as her twin daughters have both left home, now seems the ideal time. However, when Jessica and Marie turn up unexpectedly she discovers they have ideas of their own.

The Vintage Tea Room 2
room for a small one

Jessica and Edward have bought the Cotswold tea room from her mum. With their first baby due in less than a month Jessica is keen to make it their own and decides to offer a range of Artisan breads. With no experience of baking and little time to practise her first attempt does not go well.

Her mum and sister, Marie, are a little worried that Jessica has not started preparing for the arrival of the baby – she hasn't even bought a cot. However, Jessica is determined to get this new aspect to their business up and running before the baby arrives.

Christmas in Cornwall

Heather has planned the best Christmas ever. She is going to spend Christmas Day with Nick, they are going to commit to their relationship and, finally, she will be able to introduce him as her boyfriend.

One phone call from her sister and her plans are thrown into disarray when Heather has to hot foot it down to Cornwall to help Sarah look after the children. She loves spending time with her nephew and niece but is worried that Nick doesn't seem keen to answer her texts or phone calls. As long as she can get back home on Christmas Eve she should still be able to get her plans back on track.

Printed in Great Britain
by Amazon

85452663R00058